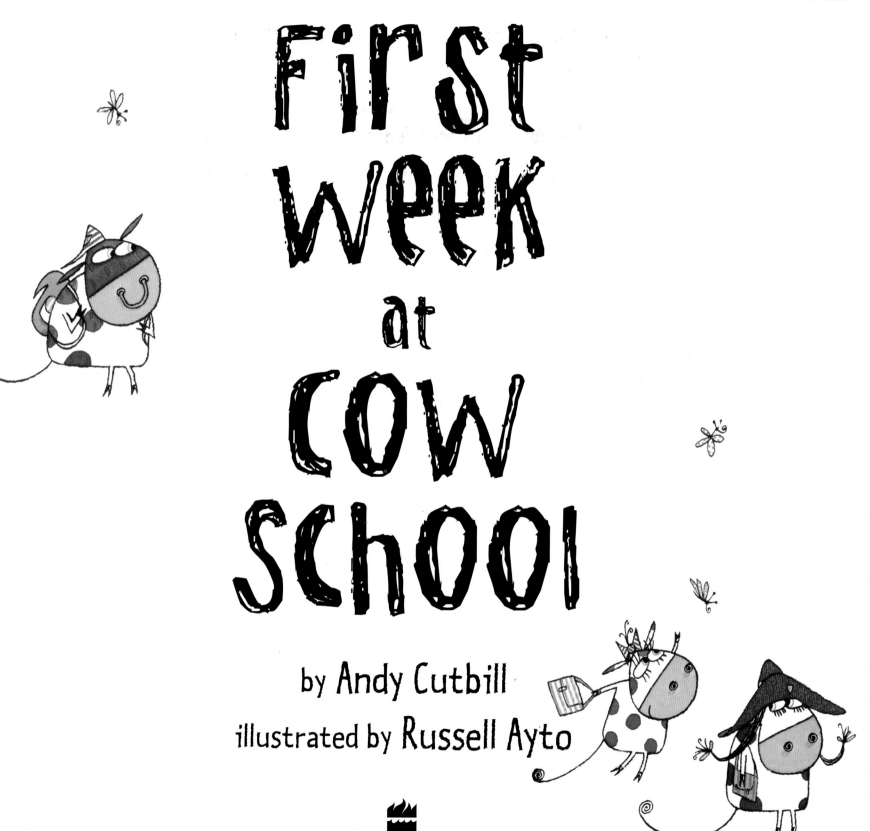

First week at Cow School

by Andy Cutbill

illustrated by Russell Ayto

HarperCollins *Children's Books*

It was Monday morning. Marjorie the cow was just straightening Daisy's ribbons when...

ing-a-ling!

The farmyard bell rang.
"Welcome to Cow School, children,"
trilled Miss Gold-Top, the teacher.

Marjorie was feeling jolly proud.

It seemed only yesterday that her daughter had amazed everyone by hatching from an egg!

MOOS OF THE WORLD

COW LAYS EGG!

THE DAILY TITTLE-CATTLE

HOLY COW! ITS HATCHED

MOTHER AND BABY

Eggstraordinary Baby !!!

Just then the chickens popped up.

"Good luck, Daisy," they called.

Daisy gave her mum a kiss and skipped inside.

"Now," said Miss Gold-Top. "Let's start with a bit of **hOOf** painting."

All the cows got stuck in straight away.

Soon there were great big **splodgy** pictures everywhere.

But Daisy's picture was a little...*different.*

The next day was Tuesday.

"**COWPAT** Training," sang Miss Gold-Top.

All the small cows jumped straight to it.

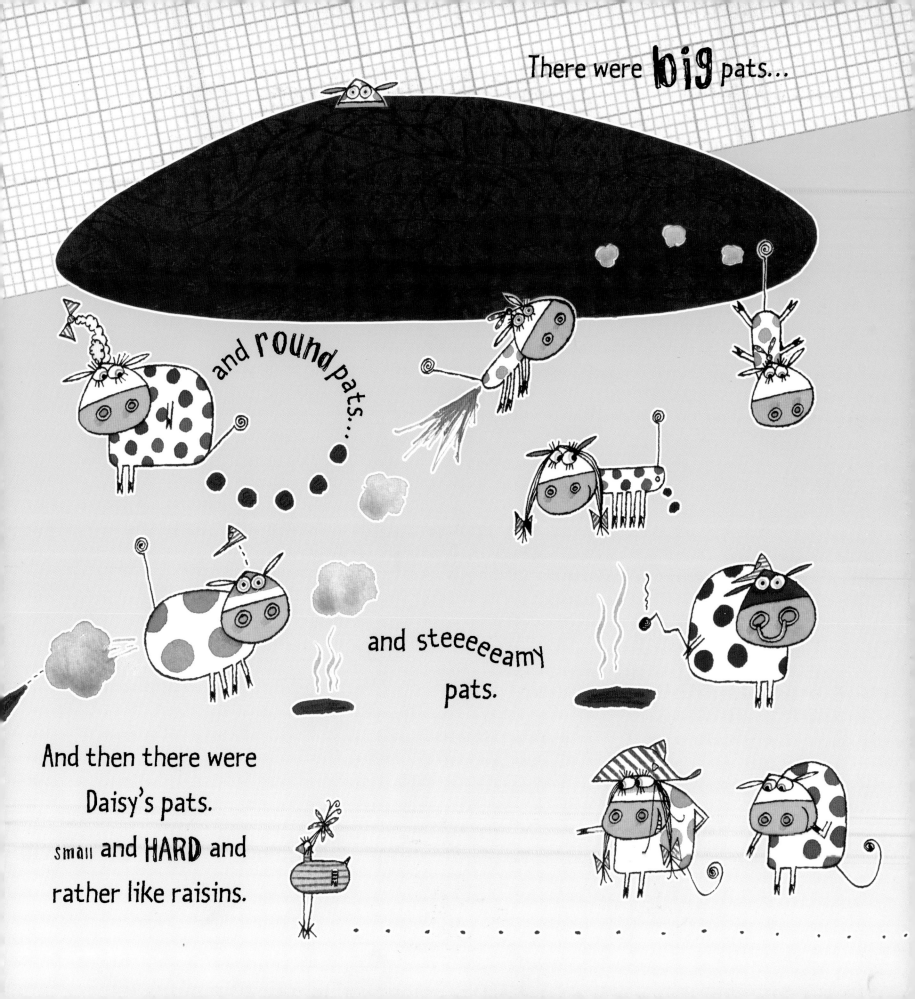

There were **big** pats...

and round pats...

and steeeeeamy pats.

And then there were Daisy's pats. small and **HARD** and rather like raisins.

On Wednesday, there was a **Cud Chewing** lesson.

All the cows stampeded into the yard and immediately started chomping.

But chomping
somehow wasn't
Daisy's cup
of tea...

BOK!

Thursday was **MOOSiC** and **MOOVEMENT**.

"Swish those tails," said Miss Gold-Top.
"Swat those flies."

All the little cows had
a marvellous time.

Swish

swish

Swish

But Daisy's tail wasn't
really long enough to swish.

Besides, she preferred
to eat the flies.

On the way home, Daisy was looking a little glum.

"What's up?" asked Marjorie.
"All the other cows are so talented," said Daisy, "but I don't feel very cow-like **at all**."

Just then the chickens popped up.
"Not very cow-like?" they spluttered.
"We'll soon
see about that!"

First thing on Friday morning, the chickens had a
very important pow-wow in Miss Gold-Top's office.

Everyone
tried to listen at
the door.

Finally Miss Gold-Top emerged. "Today," she said, a little shaken, **"flying lessons!"**

Well, the whole class was dumbstruck. No one had ever told them about flying.

Soon there were cows charging **everywhere...**

hopping up...

and down...

flapping their hooves wildly.

And not one got an inch off the ground.

Apart from...

... and landed on her bottom with a ...

BONK!

Everyone was completely gobsmacked.
So was Daisy, in fact.

"Well, bless my soul," gasped Miss Gold-Top.

"Daisy Can Fly!"

Marjorie rushed into
the classroom.

"What a **talent**,"
she whooped, scooping
up her baby.

"You'll be the most talked-about cow in history," clucked the chickens, relieved.

Daisy smiled at her mum. "Yes," she said. "Although, when I grow up, I'd like to be…

a **Chicken!**"

"Now that *would* be something special," cooed Marjorie.

And she promptly got a peck on the cheek.